The Card Slingers of the Biloxi Royale

Christian Vanderline

Table of Contents

Dedication / Copyright / Disclaimer

To Scott. You left this world too soon, my friend. In the end, you tragically became what you loved the most, ...a sad country song.

"Fortune is like glass; the brighter the
glitter, the more easily broken."
-Publius Syrus (Maxim 280. 1ˢᵗ Century BC)

Chapter 1. – Desperation Leads the Lost Soul.

Alan sat alone in the truck contemplating on what he was about to do. It was a quarter 'til five as he killed the engine in the baking afternoon sun. He glanced across the sidewalk at the entrance of the old cinderblock pawn shop just a few steps away and was torn between thoughts of desperation.

He looked at the shiny nickel plated .357 revolver tucked into the seat beside him. He grabbed a blue bandana and wiped the sweat from his eyes and glanced into the rearview mirror as he pulled his cap down low. His eyes were filled with worry and fatigue. His vision darkened as he slid a pair of mirrored sunglasses on.

Hanging from the rearview mirror, was a blue turquoise cross that his girlfriend, Cynthia, had given him to keep him safe. He reached up and tapped it with his finger as it swung back and forth.

He took a deep breath as he focused to get his nerve up; it was now or never because the pawn shop was fixing to close. He knew damn well that Cynthia wouldn't understand and that there was no way in hell he could keep her from finding out, but he had to do something to get ahead.

"Goddammit." He grumbled, as he covered the pistol up with the bandana, got out, and went around the truck. He pulled a guitar and amp from the passenger side and walked inside. As they were closing, he walked back out with a thousand bucks wadded up in his pocket, but left part of his heart back inside the old dusty shop.

The thousand bucks wouldn't knock a dent in the debt he was in, but it may take the heat off for a few days, so he could figure something out.

He got back into his truck and drove aimlessly east towards Biloxi on the beach highway. His hope began to sink like the summer sun to his back. As he reached Biloxi, the casinos towered over the flat landscape like pillars in the eastern sky.

Before he reached the end of town, he saw the flashing sign of the 'Biloxi Royale' casino.

He started to keep driving, but had an overwhelming impulse to hit the brakes and pull in. The lot had plenty of empty spots, so he was able to get one not too far from the door.

He got out, pulled down the brim of his cap and walked to the main entrance as a salty, gulf breeze filled the warm air. An orange ambient glow from the setting sun and the cries of the gulls overhead, gave a brief feeling of serenity. A security guard on the inside politely opened the dark-tinted glass door and held it for him as he walked in.

"Good luck, sir." He said, with a friendly smile.

"Thanks." Alan said, as the sound of his footsteps echoed in the empty lobby.

He knew it was probably a mistake being at the grind house, but he was desperate, and like many other fools before him, he chose to take a chance on the 'House'.

He'd played before, didn't do too well, but still wanted to give it a shot. Who knows, even a blind hog can find an acorn every now and then.

As he walked through the second set of doors, the peace and warmth of the outside quickly diminished into the chaotic atmosphere of ringing machines, and flashing lights. He followed a winding path that led through a labyrinth of slot and poker machines and eventually ended up at the table games. The smooth felt tops were all colored in a deep dark red. The ambiance of the light put off a slightly warmer glow over the pit as a slight fog hung high above them.

Monday was a slow night, so even the tables that were open were thin on players. As he walked past a few tables trying to get a feel, the only eyes that seemed to make contact were the brief nods of the dealers as he slowly passed.

He spotted a guy at pit one, table four by himself at a double deck pitch game. He'd played at the regular blackjack tables before, but never pitch. The table limit was higher than the others, but there was something about this guy that intrigued him.

He appeared to be in his late fifties; early sixties, had a worn chiseled look in his face with dark piercing eyes and greying dark hair that was shoulder length and combed back. He had an average build and a short, salt and pepper, week old beard. He resembled an aging mobster and wore a black and white untucked bowling shirt. He had a gold watch, rings, and a chain with a cross around his neck.

As Alan watched, he realized that the guy never gave a second thought or hesitation on his decisions. He had the confidence and precision of a gunslinger. The second he picked up the cards, a decision was made; he either tucked it, scraped it or flipped it over. The dealer was in constant motion to keep up with his play. It was back and forth, over and over; he'd win, then lose, win, then lose. He had several large stacks of black and green chips and few purples.

Alan stood quietly off to the side trying to get the nerve up to sit down. He was afraid he may make the guy angry if he walked into the game but felt that he'd have a better chance if he played with a seasoned player, and this guy seemed to fit the bill.

"Ya gonna stand over my shoulder like a fuckin' buzzard, or ya gonna sit down?" The guy said with his back to him, in a deep tone with a slight southern accent.

Alan quickly looked at the dealer in surprise as he shuffled the cards and glared back at him. He immediately felt awkward and out of place.

"I, ...I'm sorry." Alan said. I didn't mean to—"

"Shut up and sit down, 'Slim'." The old guy said, with a deep chuckle in his voice.

"Besides, this bottom dealin' son of a bitch takes forever and a fuckin' day to shuffle two crooked goddamn decks of cards."

The dealer glanced at both of them with frustration and continued to shuffle.

With slight reluctance, Alan pulled out the chair at the last spot on the five-spot pitch table.

"What the fuck are you doing!" The man erupted.

"You told me to sit down."

"Not on third base! You tryin' to screw us both?" He said as he turned and looked at Alan with a sigh. "Jesus Christ, we got a green horn, don't we? You've never played this game have ya, Slim?

"I've played the six deck shoes, just never pitch and I—"

"You mean you played the sucker tables; fuckin' amateur." The guys said as he turned back forward and focused on the cards.

"You know what? ...Fuck this." Alan said as he pulled his cap down and pushed the chair back in and started walking away. "My day's been hell already, I definitely don't need this shit."

"Come back and sit down." The guy said loud enough for Alan to hear.

Alan paused, as he thought about the cash in his pocket being his last desperate chance to save himself.

"I tell ya what, Slim," The man said, facing the dealer and leaving his circle empty so the dealer couldn't start. "You keep on walking, but remember, they opened the damn door for ya with a smile when you walked in with cash in your pocket; when you walk out broke later on, they're gonna make ya open the fuckin' door yourself."

Alan sighed, shook his head, and walked back over. "Ok, where the hell do I sit?"

The guy sarcastically waved his hand over the seat to his right. Alan conceded and sat down. "My name's 'Alan', mister." He said as he reached out to shake the guys hand in an attempt to reset the atmosphere.

"Name's Joel, Joel Johnson." The guy answered as he reached over and gave Alan a firm shake with Johnny walker on his breath. "Nice to meet ya, Slim."

Alan took out the crumpled wad of cash from his pocket. The dealer gave him half black and half green in return. Alan placed two greens in his circle and sat there nervously.

"Whoa!" Joel said as the dealer was about to start. "Table minimum's twenty-five; don't start bettin' fifty on the first damn hand out the shoe."

Joel's outburst drew the attention of the pit boss, Jake Goldman. Jake was an old school floor manager. He was in his sixties; a grindhouse veteran from casinos from Nevada and Jersey. He was a big guy, cleaned cut, trimmed mustache and intimidating personality. He knew every trick in the book because he's seen every trick in the book. The casino valued him as the guy that always kept the 'house' in order.

As Jake walked up to the table, Joel cut his eye towards him.

"Joel, you know the rules," Jake said. "You can't tell the other player's what to do."

"I know the fuckin' rules, Jake." Joel answered with no fear. "Most of 'em were made because of me."

"It, ...It's Ok." Alan said, trying to avoid a scene.

"See there." Joel said jokingly. "It's ok, besides, ...right now, ...Slim here is the only friend I've got left."

Alan's eyes widened with that thought and a slight smile grew on his troubled face.

Since Alan had the first play, he nervously looked at Joel and saw how he picked up his cards carefully by the corner's, looked at them at a slight tilt so Alan could see that he had a hard seventeen and quickly slid his cards under his bet. Alan carefully mimicked Joel's action.

Alan had a hard sixteen, ten-six, and out of fear of busting, he did the same thing.

"Pick that shit back up." Joel said low out of the corner of his mouth. Alan quickly pulled the cards back and held them, not knowing what to do.

"It's a bust hand." Alan said.

"Sir, you can't pick up the cards once you lay them down." The dealer said sternly to Alan.

"Keep your shirt on, killer." Joel said to the dealer. "He's new at this."

Then Joel leaned towards Alan and said, "He's got a face showin' and besides that, it's the first damn cards out the shoe so the lucky bastard's probably gonna make a fuckin' hand anyway."

The dealer gave Joel a smart-ass grin, then looked to Alan for the first play.

"Now hit that goddamn sixteen!" Joel said.

Alan took a hit and frowned as the hand was busted by a face card.

The next hand out, Alan had an Ace-Ten, Blackjack. Joel leaned back and peeked over and saw it.

"Turn that shit over, Slim; if you got it and he don't, ya gotta flip it." He said. "Make sure that son of a bitch pays ya right, too; never trust these six-fingered bastards."

"Floor!" The dealer yelled as he angrily stared at Joel.

"What?" Joel asked, with a half grin.

The pit boss quickly returned. "I mean it, Joel; keep it up and see what happens."

"Yeah, yeah." He said as he gulped down his last swig. "Where's that damn waitress?"

"I'm right here, Mr. Joel." A sweet voice said, as a cute little Philippino waitress replaced his glass with another Johnny Walker red label.

"Thank you, baby." Joel gently replied with a friendly smile as he dropped a red five-dollar chip on her tray.

"Good luck to you, Mr. Joel." She said with a genuine smile, then turned to Alan. "Can I get something for you, sir."

"Yeah, I'll have a Miller Lite." He said.

"The hell he will!" Joel said, as he picked up his cards. "He'll have a coffee, black. He's got a long night ahead and we already got one too many drunk assholes on this table."

The girl gave Alan a look of inquiry, not wanting to argue.

"Coffee'll be fine." Alan said to her with a polite smile, just to pacify Joel.

Then Alan picked up his cards and saw he had a hard seventeen. Without thinking, he scraped the hand towards him for a hit. The dealer quickly reacted and dealt a face card. Alan frowned at the mistake and threw the busted hand over.

"What the hell!" Joel yelled out of surprise when he realized what he did. Not only did that bust Alan, but Joel needed that ten for a double down on an eleven hand he was holding. "Are you fuckin' insane, you never hit a hard-ass seventeen!"

"Ok, calm down, man." Alan said.

"Calm down! That's why they call it a Goddamn 'mother-in-law' hand; you wanna hit it but ya can't!"

The pit boss quickly showed up once again, except this time they were also met with a security guard from behind.

12

"That's it, Joel, we've had about enough!" The pit boss said.

Then suddenly Alan spoke up as he placed a new bet. "He can say what he wants, as long as he's talking to me." Then immediately they shrugged and left. Alan was starting to understand how things worked.

"If you're waiting for a thank you, you're not gonna get one." Joel said as he tucked his cards under hit bet.

"Not lookin' for one."

"Look, Slim." Joel said as he lit a cigarette. "If you're in here just to have a little fun and blow off some steam by losing a thousand bucks, let me know now, because I'm not wasting my time ridin' a train that's gonna run out of track."

"I need the money, ok." Alan said low, angrily and upset as he stared forward. "Besides, you don't know shit about me."

"Ok, ok." Joel said, trying to hush him as the dealer made his play, and like Alan, he lost his hand too.

The next hands came out and they both stayed on stiff hands. Then again, like a recurring bad dream, the dealer made a winner out of a bust card. Alan's already low confidence was deteriorating, and the silence made it more awkward.

"I shouldn't even fuckin' be in here." Alan said, as he watched the dealer take his bet. "Probably just another stupid thing I'll kick myself for later, but what the hell, I ain't got nothin' to lose anymore, anyhow."

"Mr. Alan, we play by the same rules as you." The dealer said, trying to reassure him.

"Don't listen to that shit, Slim." Joel said to Alan while giving the dealer a cold stare. "If you bust and this card jockey busts, he wins; not quite the same rules. He's got no skin in the game and no choices; you do."

Alan's hands began to shake, but as he watched Joel take a sip from his glass, he noticed he was cool as ice and balanced. Nothing seemed to shake this guy up; he was relentlessly unsettled.

Alan, visibly upset, stared at the table and took a deep breath.

"Calm down, Slim" Joel said as he held his chips, but then paused on putting his bet in the circle.

Alan glanced at his dwindling stacks of chips as the house edge began to take its bite.

"Meet me in the west restroom." Joel said low as he set his chips down, shot his last swig and got up. "It's the only place in here where the eye in the sky ain't hawking over us."

Alan perked up quickly and looked around in confusion but did as he asked and stood up.

Joel tapped his spot, so the dealer would lock it with a glass chip. As he stood behind his chair, he joked at the pit boss. "When you gonna put my sign on my chair, Jake!"

"When hell freezes over, Joel." Jake, the pit boss, yelled back from the pit.

"Years of sitting in this chair more than anyone, and they still won't put my name on it." Joel said with a grin, then framed his hands behind it. "It should say, 'Reserved for Joel Johnson.'." Then he laughed, nudged at Alan and they walked away.

"Love him or hate him," Jake said to the dealer as Joel and Alan walked away, "You gotta give it to the son of a bitch, he's definitely one of a kind."

"Yeah, well, regardless, he's still a son of a bitch." The dealer said with a sour face.

Chapter 2. – The Shadows behind the Neon.

In the privacy of the large restroom, Alan glanced in the mirror at his stress filled, blood-shot eyes. Joel takes off his two gold rings and washes his face. One was a horseshoe and the other had a diamond studded cross on it.

"Kind of an odd pair don't ya think?" Alan said, looking at the rings.

"You're tellin' me, Slim." Joel said as he wiped his face dry. "Oh, you mean the rings?" Then put them back on. "One's for luck, and the other's for life."

"Hope the horseshoe's for luck." He said. "What about the other?"

"Been wearin' that my whole life; the horseshoe, just for when I play."

"For someone who likes to play so much, you sure do hate the 'House'." Alan replied.

"What's to like about it, Slim? you're in the 'devil's' house; everything's about illusion and confusion. Every trick the devil can play happens right here. No clocks or windows on the walls, anything you want, they make it happen to keep you here." He said, then looked Alan in the eye as if he could see through him. "And they won't stop 'til they get it all."

"Well, they can only get so much out of me." Alan responded. "I ain't got much to lose."

"Still got your soul." Joel said as he looked back in the mirror and wiped his face dry.

The remark put Alan at a brief pause.

"The lights, the sounds, the smells; all designed to get into your head. Even the carpet's twisted and confusing; everything's intentional and bears a mark."

"Everything?" Alan said, being skeptical.

"Everything." He said as he threw the paper towel in the garbage and put his rings back on. "When ya get bored, add up the numbers on that roulette wheel at the end of the pit and see what it adds up to; there's nothing coincidental here."

"So?"

"So, if you wanna win, you have to be careful not to get caught in their game. You gotta squeeze the odds and understand how to read the cards and the people. Play slow and don't get greedy. And above all else, if you find yourself playing the way they want you to play, then you're playing wrong."

"But I'm losing every—"

"And that's another thing, Slim." He said. "No matter what, never, ...*ever*, show emotion at the table. Never let 'em see ya sweat; don't give the cock-suckers the satisfaction."

"How the hell are you shaving the odds and staying even?" Alan asked.

"Every card they deal changes the odds, the deeper in the deck, the easier it is to figure the odds on the next card. It's only a small edge, so ya have to play each hand right and be careful not to fuck it up."

"You counting cards like in those books?"

"Those goddamn books are written for suckers; I count, but I count for the play, not the spreads." Joel said. "You don't learn what I do from no fuckin' books, I guarantee ya that shit."

"So, how do I know—"

"You don't have to know, leave that up to me." Joel said. "Just trust me, win or lose, you're gonna have better chances."

"You just don't want me to screw you up again, do ya?"

"Well, ...yeah, that too." He said, "Now let's get back out there before they cage our chips."

"If you don't mind me asking, how come you're such an ass to everyone?" Alan asked jokingly, not wanting to leave quite so fast.

"Two reasons. Number one, it throws 'em off. The personality hides the strategy. They focus on that and nothing else; keeps 'em at bay."

"What's the other reason?"

"Number two," He said with a confused pause, then smiled. "...Maybe I'm just kind of an ass."

"Can't argue with that." Alan said with a shrug.

They walked out of the restroom and onto the twisted carpet as they made their way through the maze of slots and video poker machines back to the table.

"I got a long damn way to go to get where I need to be." Alan said.

"What happened, ya miss a car payment?"

"Car payment? Shit, I wish; I'm so far behind on everything I'd need a miracle to catch up."

"What you do for a living?"

"Musician." He said. "I pawned my guitar and amp for the money, but I knew it wouldn't be near enough to get me in the clear, so here I am."

"You married?"

"No, got a girlfriend." He said. "She doesn't even know I'm here."

They reached the table and Joel quickly changed his train of thought.

"Goddamn, Jake!" Joel roared jokingly to the pit boss, "You don't have a sign on my chair yet? I want it in big, bold, red letters!"

Jake just frowned, shook his head and walked away.

The waitress came and went again; Coffee, Johnny Walker Red Label and a five-dollar tip on the tray. An action that became routine.

"Hey, Joel." The young dealer said sarcastically. "How about that tip for the dealer? You know, that guy that's dealing those winning hands? Maybe one day you'll shock us all and at least do a dealer bet."

"You stand as good of a chance at getting a tip out of me as I do of getting that sign on my chair." Joel said. "Not gonna happen; besides, you ain't got shit to do with the way the cards come out. If ya did, you wouldn't be dealing."

"See why all the dealer's love this fuckin' guy?" The dealer said to Alan with a smirk.

As the next few shoes were dealt, Alan started to get lucky as he caught a slight swing.

"Hell, yeah!" He said after winning a split for a double.

"Don't get cocky, Slim." Joel said low. "Even a broken watch is right twice a day. Don't take chances when you're feeling lucky. You're not playing for the next hand, you're playing for a slight edge of the next couple o' hundred hands."

"Yeah, well, it feels better than losing every hand." Alan replied.

"It's just a swing; the odds at work. What goes up must come down." Joel said. "Like the law of gravity, it's back and forth."

Alan started to understand what Joel was talking about. It was like a silent language in the cards. Joel was obviously hardened to the cruel cycles and never showed any emotion. Maybe this was how he got under the skin of the house? He'd sit for hours, on their time, drinking house whiskey and putting them on edge while careful not to add any stake in the game other than what the swings would allow.

The shoe ended, and Alan was gaining a little more confidence. Then suddenly another player walked up and threw a yellow plastic card across the table, laid a couple of hundred-dollar bills ahead of the first base circle, then sat down. He was the type of person Joel described earlier. Someone probably passing through, killing time and win or lose, just in it for a good time. He was the yuppie type, golf shirt, highlighted hair, mid-forties and a real prick.

"New shuffle, fellas?" The stranger asked, cheerfully.

"New barrel of fuckin' monkeys!" Joel said ferociously as if he was angry that the new player came into the game. "Where's my girl!" He added, as he looked around for the waitress.

Alan watched as the floor manager came over and looked at the card and entered information into the computer next to the dealer. Then he threw it back to the man and said, "Good luck to you, Mr. Richard"

"What's that card he gave them?" Alan said, leaning towards Joel.

"You don't have a player's card?" Joel asked.

Alan shook his head 'no' in confusion.

"Jake!" Joel yelled.

Alan made an expression as if he wasn't so sure it was a good idea to ask.

Jake looked up from the center pit, took a sigh and walked over.

"What now, Joel?"

"How come you didn't ask Slim for a card?" Joel asked. "You guys so hard up for cash, ya screwin' the new blood on wagers?"

Jake ignored Joel's sarcasm and got Alan's driver's license information and threw a red card across the table to him.

"How come mine's red and his is yellow." Alan asked.

"Because he's and old fool like me, Slim." Joel said as the cards once again started to fly. "And there's no fool like and old fool."

"What's the card for?" Alan asked again with persistence.

"You'll find out later, Slim." Joel said with a deep breath as he picked up his hand. "Right now, stay focused; You're fuckin' killin' me over here."

As the shoe ended, Alan asked Joel. "How come they call everyone 'Mister', but by first name? Sounds kinda funny in a way."

"Anonymity." Joel answered sarcastically as he lit a cigarette.

Then Jake interjected into the conversation, "'Mr. Alan' is all we know you as. Some people don't want others to know who they are while they're in here. It's not such a bad thing when ya think about it."

"No, I guess not." Alan answered. "Not a bad thing at all."

"Well that's all fine and dandy," Joel said, as he placed his bet and exhaled.

"What, Joel?" Jake said. "Ya got a problem with that too?"

"No, but you should inform Slim that the anonymity only goes so far."

"How so?" Alan asked.

"Because in a week or so, your significant other is gonna know exactly where you've been when they send you a stupid fuckin' mailer with chump change offers, thanking you for losing your ass."

"What!" Alan replied, then looked across the table at Jake. "Is that true?"

"Why ya think they got a copy your license?" Joel said.

"Goddammit, Joel!" Jake said as he threw up his hands and walked away in disgust.

Joel grinned and chuckled as he shot down a swig of whiskey and shook his head. He peeked at his hand, scraped the cards for a hit then tucked them under his bet and said calmly, "Slim, I told ya once whose house this is; ya got no friends on the other side of the table. Don't ever buy into their bullshit con. That's how it starts."

The dealer rolled his eyes at the statement and played out his hand in disgust.

Jake and another floor manager, Robert Bancroft, met in the pit. Robert was young and new to the floor. Like all floor personnel, he came from dealing the tables. He was bright and eager to please, but still green compared to the seasoned, hardnosed Jake.

"Look at that son of a bitch, would ya." Jake said, referring to Joel. "how we sittin'?"

"He's up more than a grand, ...but, ...like always, he's back and forth."

"Bastards been here since yesterday; he's run off every player except for this new chump."

"He's a time player; careful and calm." Robert said.

"I know what the fuck he is! He's an asshole, that's what he is." Jake snapped, then calmed himself. "You guys just stay on him tight; every second he's here now, even if he's even, we're at a loss."

"He sure seemed to hit it off with that guy." Robert answered, referring to Alan. "Ya think he's a friend of his? They may be up to something."

"No, that guys a fuckin' chump, we'll get his money before the sun comes up." Jake answered. "Besides, you ever know Joel Johnson to have any friends?"

"Nope."

"Make sure to keep him from pissin' off first base until he's at a loss of at least three hundred."

"Mr. Richard?"

"Yeah, 'yuppie' Richard." Jake said. "We got him in for three hundred and he's up around a hundred bucks. As soon as he loses that and buys back in, back off of Joel. Richard will eventually get tired of his shit and leave. He's always an easy take for a few hundred."

"What about Mr. Alan?"

"He came in with a grand, but he's new and that makes him unpredictable." Jake said. "We'll start squeezin' his ass as soon as he get's a little lower. Never take a chance on beginner's luck."

Chapter 3. – The Weight of the Grind.

3♣

As they played on through the night and the floor shifted from swing to graveyard, the money was back and forth. Stress and fatigue were taking its toll on Alan as he eventually lost his gain and was down to half of the grand he started with.

Unfortunately for Alan, the loss also caught the attention of the floor and they quickly focused on him.

It was a cruel, vicious cycle that seemed to go on and on; A tense mood that made him feel doomed, like he'd never get back ahead. Strange how the 'House' gives false hope then knocks you back down. The back and forths, and ups and downs create a twisted depression. In his sleep deprived mind, the faces of the floor and dealers started to morph into something dark and sinister.

It was enough to make Alan want to go for broke at times and throw it all on the line just to stop the mental torture. And if not for Joel, he probably would. Win or lose, it would put him out of his misery.

Richard, the guy on first base finally lost his gain, caught a bad swing, over-bet out of anxiety and busted out. He bought back in for another two hundred and his mood began to change as that started to dwindle as well.

Alan, on Joel's signal, hit a hard twelve against a dealer four up-card.

"Hey buddy," Richard said to Alan. "Ya wanna ease up on hitting against the bust cards?"

"What?"

"You keep taking the dealer's bust cards; I'm down almost a half a grand here."

"Hey, man. I'm sorry if—"" Alan said.

"Who the fuck do you think you are!" Joel quickly lashed back at Richard.

"Whoa." Alan said trying to avoid the floor's attention.

"Even the book says to stay on that hand." Richard said, trying to defend his words.

"The fuckin' book?" Joel said with sarcasm.

Richard pulled out a small plastic card with the basic strategy chart for blackjack and said, "Yeah, says right here that—"

"Who gives a fuck what your card says?" Joel roared. "If that shit actually worked, they wouldn't let ya have it at the table. They even sell 'em for a buck in every casino gift shop. Ya ever wonder why?"

"Hey, I'm just saying, we're all on the same team on this side of the table."

"Ok, cool." Joel said. "Since we're on the same team, give me half your chips."

"What? Dude, look—"

"No, you fuckin' look, Pal." Joel said. "You play your fuckin' cards, we'll play ours, you got a fuckin' problem with that?"

The floor stood back at a distance and watched, and by Jakes direction, they were sure to not intervene.

"You know what?" Richard said nervously. "I'm out of here. Fuck this shit." Then he slid his last few chips to the dealer. "Color me up."

After Richard left, Joel leaned over to Alan and said, "Cock sucker had no idea that the cards left in the deck were small."

Alan exhaled nervously, pulled his cap low, and glanced over towards the floor to see if they were looking.

30

"Relax, Slim; they don't give a shit." Joel said. "They were ready for him to pack up for the night anyhow; they had him at a good loss and didn't want to chance another swing."

"The card, the basic strategy," Alan asked. "Why *do* they allow it?"

"Because it keeps 'em in the game longer; let's them lose at a slower pace so they don't lose too fast."

"Too fast?" Alan said.

"I asked a casino manager in New Orleans one night why he liked to see folks lose slow." Joel said. "His response was, 'You can sheer a sheep many times, but you can only slaughter it once.'"

"So they think they had a chance, when in fact, they didn't." Alan said as it made more sense.

"That's right." Joel said. "But get ready, because you're startin' to get to a spot where you're gonna feel the weight of the grind jus' like that preppie cock-sucker that jus' bailed."

Since Richard left, and it was just the two of them again, the cards did seem to get a little better, but Alan once again started to slip back into the hypnotic drone of the agonizing repetition.

Even though there were only two decks in the shoe and it only got half played before each shuffle, the cycle went on infinitely. The rhythm of the cards played to the old playlist of non-stop cheap music and relentless ringing of machines. It was like a nightmare; he imagined an ocean of cards that constantly flew from the dealer's hand and across the dark, deep, blood red felt like waves that went in and out, over and over, wins and losses.

"You ok, Slim?" Joel asked.

"What? ...yeah." Alan said in a daze. "I'm fine."

"Ya look a little glazed."

"I'm gonna go wash my face and run to my truck and get a pack of smokes." Alan said, and suddenly disappeared.

Jake was about to get off for the night and suddenly saw Alan's empty chair and freaked. He immediately called the eye in the sky.

"Where'd the guy at table four run off too? Seat three."

32

"Stand by." The guy on the phone answered. After a slight delay, he replied. "He's coming back into the interior doors of the lobby right now." He said. "Looks like he's stopping to talk to someone—".

"I see him." Jake said as he abruptly hung up and watched across the floor as Alan stopped and was talking to someone. It was a young woman in a short electric blue cocktail dress. She was brunette, dark-eyed, built and sexy as hell.

"Hey, excuse me." She said in a smooth tone. "You got a few dollars so I can grab a quick breakfast."

Alan was caught off guard and didn't know how to respond to her forwardness.

"I know it sounds bad." She added and smiled innocently. "I got caught up in the slots and didn't realize I lost every penny until I got ready to leave. I'll pay ya back."

Alan reached into his pocket and gave her his last ten bucks, wadded up and crumpled and said. "No worry; have a good morning."

"Hey thanks!" She said. "You busy? If you want, you can—"

Alan didn't even wait to see what she had to say, he was focused on getting back to the table.

Joel caught Jakes stare off to the entrance and slowly looked over with squinted eyes and a caught a glimpse of the brief interaction.

"Oh Shit." He said softly to himself with frustration.

As Alan got closer, Joel turned and focused back on the cards.

Alan sat down and opened a new pack of cigarettes as the waitress set down a fresh cup of coffee.

"Ya ok?" Joel asked.

Alan looked at Joel and just nodded as he got back into the game.

"They're watchin' ya, Slim." Joel said low as he stared forward.

"How ya know?"

"Trust me; I know." Joel answered as he picked up his hand, glanced at a pair of faces and tucked them.

Alan shrugged if off as Joel being paranoid.

The back and forth turned and Alan started to finally get a slight gain back.

Then the pit phone rang, and Jake walked over to the table and stopped the dealer while he listened to the eye in the sky for instructions.

"Ok." Jake said into the phone, then looked up at Alan.

"The hell's goin' on?" Alan asked Joel.

"Jus' be cool." Joel said. "This is where they're gonna try ya."

"What?"

"Mr. Alan." Jake said as he lowered the phone. "During the previous shoe, the dealer paid you on a push."

"So?"

"So, ...you owe the casino fifty dollars on a bet you didn't win. They have it all on video."

For the first time, Alan showed aggression. Joel smiled and leaned back knowing that this was proof of what he had been trying to teach him.

"Show me the video!" Alan exclaimed.

"That's not gonna happen." Jake said with a smug look. "Now, you can either give us two green chips or, you can be escorted to the door and be banned; it's up to you."

Then Jake waved and security showed up behind Alan's chair.

"What the hell; you can't do that!" Alan said, then looked at Joel. "Can they do that?"

"Yep." Joel said. "And you'll be arrested on the spot if you ever come back for illegally trespassing. Even if you're not playing."

"That's right, friend." Jake said, still holding the phone. "And we can ban you for any reason we feel like; maybe you should check the state gaming laws."

"Pay 'em, Slim." Joel said. "Don't push it. They got you at a loss and right now, they're jus' trying to push you out while they're ahead."

"Stay out of this, Joel." Jake said.

"Pay 'em, Slim." Joel said, ignoring Jake's command.

"But—"

"But nothing; jus' fuckin' do it." He added.

Alan slammed down two green chips ahead of his circle, sat back with his arms folded and gritted his teeth. Jake gave security a nod, they left and the game resumed.

"Don't sweat it, Slim." Joel said. "It happens all the time."

"What if the mistake would have been to their loss and they owed me the fuckin' money?"

"They would've paid you." The dealer said, budding in.

"That's bullshit, pal." Joel said to the dealer. "All my years on these fuckin' felt-tops, not once have I ever seen the house roll back and pay a player for a mistake unless the player caught it first."

Alan finally started to realize that Joel was right, it's all smoke and mirrors; an elaborate charade designed to take and never give.

"How ya feel about the house now, Slim?" Joel said as he slowly picked up a new dealt hand and held it for a hit."

The game resumed and after more back and forth, another player, a woman, sat down at first base and the cards went sour along with the mood once again.

"Sit out a shoe, Slim." Joel said as he noticed Alan's fatigue and aggravation. "Get some more coffee and calm your nerves."

Without arguing, Alan waived the first deal of the following shoe. He could feel the void of hope and felt as if the devil had him in a tight squeeze. He looked at Joel; he was a machine. He was cold as ice and never faltered in play. Who knows, maybe it was Joel that got into his head. Curious about what Joel said about the roulette wheel earlier while in the restroom, Alan started adding up the thirty-six numbers to calm his nerves as he sat out the shoe.

"Six hundred and sixty-six!" Alan said out loud. "Are you fucking kiddin' me!"

"What! ...What's going on?" Joel asked, then saw him staring at the roulette wheel.

The woman seemed a little freaked at the outburst. The eye in the sky alerted the floor and Jake quickly showed back up.

"We got other people playing; one more scene and you're both out for the night." He looked directly at Alan and added. "That goes for you, too."

"C'mon, Slim; let's go back to the office." Joel said quietly to Alan as the shoe ended and they stood up.

Chapter 4. – Into the Graveyard.

As Alan ran warm water over his face, he looked up into the mirror at his bloodshot eyes. He was beat mentally and physically. Joel walked over from the urinal and washed his hands.

"We don't wanna rattle their cages too much." Joel said with an echo as he looked in the mirror. "These assholes on the graveyard shift were mad at the world before they ever even showed up for work. For now, just let me talk; if you see me twisting my ring, up your bet. I'll tell ya when to hit, split, double, ...whatever; they don't focus on the play as much as the bet fluctuation. Bastards have a million eyes, but they don't have any ears."

"Ya know what, Joel" Alan said in a defeated tone. "I'm fuckin' wore out and honestly, this was all another bad idea on my part. Maybe I should just cut my losses and go."

"You're already balls deep in shit, Slim." Joel said.

"So why get any deeper!" Alan said, frustrated and tired. "At least I got enough for a meal."

"You're down half a grand!" Joel yelled back. "I'm down at least a grand every damn day at some point. It's just how the swing works, nobody can help that. Besides, you put a grand on the table to start. You gonna surrender just because your half empty?"

Alan was a total wreck and stood there silent in thought. He had made up his mind but couldn't seem to shake the persistence of Joel.

"Look, Slim." Joel said. "This place isn't any different than anything else in life. When you're in the tall grass, you're either the *Lion* or the *Gazelle*. Right now, ...you're in the tall grass. So, what's it gonna be?"

"My eyes are burning, I ain't ate since yesterday, I can't go back home tonight or my girlfriend's gonna fuckin' kill me, and because of you! ...I'm so fuckin' wired on caffeine, I'm starting to see shit!"

"Hey, ya wanna cut and run, go ahead, Slim; be the gazelle." Joel answered, as he looked in the mirror and ran his fingers through his hair.

"What guarantee do I have that I can even break even, much less win."

"None; you want a guarantee, go shop at fuckin' Sears." Joel said. "But, if you wanna give it a shot and see it through, get a comp for a room and a meal; I'll see ya in eight hours and we'll give 'em hell again."

"I can do that?"

"Do what?"

"They'll just give me a room and a meal?"

"Are you fuckin' kiddin' me?" Joel answered, "On a Monday? They'd a give you two hookers and a pink fuckin' Cadillac to keep ya here. All you need is the devil's credit card."

"So that's what the player's card is for?"

"Exactly."

Alan stared in the mirror in conflicted thoughts. He didn't spend all this time just to end up on the losing end one more time but considering his run of shit luck in everything he's done recently, his confidence was hanging by a thread.

"Ok," Alan said, as he washed his eyes, "But how do we get rid of the bitch on the end of the table?"

"She's definitely screwing the hands up." Joel said as he rubbed his unshaven chin in thought. "Takes away the number of hands dealt per shoe; fucks the count up."

"So, what do we do about her; she's killin' me."

"Longneck." Joel said.

"Longneck?"

"She becomes a problem, order that Miller Lite, take one sip, put it on your right side, then tip it across the circles. Casino can't play on wet spots. That simple, but if you do, be overly apologetic and make *damn* sure it looks accidental because the eye in the sky's gonna rewind it more than a few times; won't be the first time they've seen it happen, so let's just say, they'll frown upon it. But regardless, those spots will be dead for at least two hours or more."

"I think I'll just get that comp and a room, instead." Alan said, in better spirits. "Maybe you can teach me how you do that countin' thing later?"

"Maybe later, Slim; maybe later." Joel answered as they walked out onto the twisted carpet.

"Before I forget, Slim; I gotta warn ya of somethin'" Joel said as they walked. "That gal ya ran into at the door earlier? The one in the short skirt with the unbelievable ass?"

"Yeah?"

"She hit ya up for some cash?"

"Few dollars for breakfast." Alan said as he rubbed his face trying to stay awake. "So?"

"Well that's Debbie." Joel said. "She's a hooker."

"I figured so, but so what; not like I did anything wrong."

"Not yet, Slim, but remember, they got ya on tape giving her cash. If she shows up at your room later, ...*do not let her in*." Joel said. "You understand?"

"Don't plan on it." Alan answered.

"You don't have any reason for them to shake ya down right now, but later they might, and they got cameras in the hotel hallways too. They always save it for insurance, ...Just in case."

"But I didn't do anything that—"

"Don't matter, the video tells a different story." Joel said.

"Hey, Joel." Alan asked before they reached the tables. "How come you don't ever tip or side bet for the dealer? Seems like it would be a nice gesture to keep the peace."

"Tip the fuckin' dealer!" Joel roared in aggravation, "Are you serious? And give my winnings back to the fuckin' house! No fuckin' way, Slim. When you tip the dealer, you're not just tippin' the dealer, you're tipping every asshole on the floor."

"What about the waitress you—"

"She works for it, and it goes to her, not everyone else." He said. "And, ...I like my drink on the rocks; ya tip 'em, they don't water 'em down."

When they get back to the table, Joel calls the floor manager over and gets Alan a comp for a room and a meal. Then Jake walked over to sign the comp and Alan heads to the casino restaurant to get a burger.

"Still no damn sign on my Chair?" Joel said with his normal sarcasm.

"You bring down the house, Joel." Jake said, as he walked away, "I'll see about that fuckin' sign."

Forty-five minutes later, Joel is up a few thousand, as Alan made one last pass by the table before heading up to the hotel room.

"I thought you'd be coma toast by now, Slim." Joel said, as he picked up his cards and scraped the table. "You get a meal?"

"Yeah, I feel better already." Alan said. "You're gonna be here later on, right?"

"Slim, I'm always here." He said, intensely focused on the cards.

After a few moments passed, Joel realized that Alan was still standing there.

"Go rest, man. Go; ...I'll be here." He said as he gave him a friendly fist bump on the arm. "I'm getting close to finishing with three grand, then I'm going back to a room too."

Then Joel's expression changed when he caught sight of someone past Alan walking quickly towards them from the entrance.

"Oh Shit, not now." He said with a sigh.

"What's wrong?" Alan asked.

"June." Joel said as he looked at his watch, "The hell is she doing here at this time of the morning?" Then looked back at Alan. "You better get out o' here, Slim. This ain't gonna be pretty."

"June? That your wife?"

"No, but, you, ...you really should go on and get up to your—"

"Son of a bitch!" An angry woman's voice said as it approached quickly.

"Ok, ...here we go." Joel said, as he turned back to the table and rolled his eyes.

"God dammit, Dad, you promised, you wouldn't be here." She said in a loud voice. "But I shoulda fuckin' known."

"Baby, please keep your voice down, there's people—"

"Fuck these goddamn people! They're all just bunch of fucking degenerates just like you."

Alan rolled his eyes and tried his best to get out of the middle.

June angrily slammed a bottle of prescription pills on the felt table next to Joel that he was obviously not taking.

"Go ahead and just kill yourself, Dad. Keep drinking and gambling and not giving a shit about anyone but yourself" She said. "This is the reason mom left you a long damn time ago."

Then she looked at Alan, who tried to avoid being involved. "Who the fuck is this asshole?" She said, with a piercing stare.

"Tried to warn ya, Slim." Joel said calmly as he looked away.

"I'm, ...just a friend?" Alan said, sheepishly as he held his hands up in defense.

"A friend? ...How odd, seeing that my Dad has no friends, congratulations, you are his only friend." She said, laced with sarcasm. "How great for you!"

"Actually, he mentioned that 'friend' thing earlier and—" Alan added without thinking.

The waitress walked up and suddenly, June grabbed Joel's glass of Johnny Walker from her tray and threw it in Alan's face.

"Shit!" He yelled.

Joel raised his hand to plead with the floor not to intervene.

"Both you assholes can go straight to hell." She said as she stormed off.

"Holy Shit!" Alan said as the liquor ran down his shirt. "I take it that was your—"

"Daughter, Yeah." Joel said calmly, as he watched her walk away. He had a slight look of sorrow in his face. "She takes after her mother." Then he looked back at Alan and said, "Looks like *you* got lucky though, Slim."

"Lucky? She just threw a damn drink in my damn face."

"Well, ...if you were still here sitting down, it would've been hot black coffee."

"Oh, ...that makes me feel a lot better, Joel." Alan said as he wiped his face with some drink napkins from the waitress. "You two gonna be ok, she seems a tad bit pissed."

"She'll be fine. She's done this before."

"Ok, whatever, ...I'm gone." Alan said, totally exhausted. "Eight hours, right?"

"You got it, Slim; Eight Hours." Joel said as he looked at his gold watch then back at the table. "See ya at three this afternoon."

"What?" Alan said, realizing that the casino never lets sunlight in. "Oh Jesus, It's sunrise."

Chapter 5. – The Sign.

After two hours of deep sleep and twisted nightmares, Alan could hear a light 'tap, tap, tap'. His mind was in a state of half consciousness. The sound continued as he drifted back asleep. He could see a figure at the door in his mind, but realized as he awoke again, that it must have been a dream. Maybe it was Joel's constant opinions of the house that compounded the state of paranoia.

Then suddenly "Tap, tap, tap." The sound happened again and was loud enough to thrust his mind into consciousness and his eyes popped open. His blood pressure rose as he eased out of the bed and without even looking through the peep hole, he carefully and silently eased the security latch shut and went back to sleep.

--

Six hours, a shower, a comped breakfast, a few cigarettes and two cups of coffee later, Alan walked across the floor to the pitch table at pit one. He took a deep breath and shook his head in aggravation. He noticed a sign on the back of the chair where Joel had sat all night. In bright red bold letters, just as he had joked about, were the words, 'RESERVED FOR JOEL JOHNSON.'

Only problem was that Joel wasn't there as he promised.

The waitress from the day before was back on her shift and quickly appeared.

"You need some coffee, baby?" She asked in a sympathetic tone.

"Coffee sounds fine. Thanks." Alan said low, as if he had been abandoned.

All the sudden there he was, Joel abruptly sat down in his chair. Sleep seemed to do him well also.

"Sorry, I'm a few minutes late, Slim; got tied up with some bullshit earlier." Then looked at the waitress and said, "No liquor for me today, Sweetheart! Pass me on by. We got some 'House' cleanin' to do, me and Slim."

The waitress noted the coffee, smiled and walked away.

Alan grinned ear to ear. He was still at a loss, but somehow, he felt better just knowing that Joel showed back up like he promised.

"Finally got your sign, huh?" Alan said with a laugh.

"Yeah, these jerkoffs are bunch of fuckin' smartasses." Joel answered as he leaned behind to look at the paper sign that was scotch-taped to his chair. "At least they spelled my name right."

"How'd you do last night after I left?"

"Let's just say, It got bad for a while after you left, but then, it got better." He said, enthusiastically. "So today, Slim, we worry about you. Let's focus and see if we can get you where you need to be."

Jake wasn't due back until later that evening, which left the day shift floor manager and the new guy, Robert from the night before, in control of the floor. Alan, as well as the dealers were relieved; at least the unbearable tension between Jake and Joel wasn't present.

"Mr. Alan." The dealer said, as the shift floor manager stood beside him. "We just wanted to say that we're sorry about how things went yesterday."

"Yeah, well, ...It did suck pretty bad, but thanks. Hopefully today will be much better."

As the dealer shuffled the deck, Alan kept looking ahead and whispered to Joel. "Sorry about you and your daughter last night. I hope ya'll get things worked out."

"June? She'll be fine." Joel said. "I'm gonna see her again first thing in the morning."

"Yeah?" Alan said. "Hope it goes better than it did this morning."

"That's why we gotta wrap things up." He said as he looked at his gold watch. "Let's just be cool and bring the fuckin' house down. We're gonna play for higher stakes so be calm and focus on the cards. Don't pay attention to me or they'll bust our asses out of here; listen to me on the plays and watch my ring for the bets."

"Where's your cross ring, Joel." Alan asked, noticing that Joel was only wearing the gold horseshoe ring.

"It's in my pocket, Slim." Joel answered. "I don't want to confuse you; now pay attention, we don't have all fuckin' day."

"You know what, Joel?" Alan said. "You're not such asshole when you're sober."

"Yeah, well ...jus' don't go getting' used to it, Slim."

After a few hours of back and fourth play, the table had players come in and out, but eventually the two sat there alone again. Alan had gotten skilled at watching Joel's hand for bets and listening for the right plays. Eventually, the tables had turned, and the swing went in his favor.

Then someone sat at first and the next few hands turned on them again. He was a rough looking guy that played for himself. He hit bust hands when the deck was stacked with high cards against dealer bust cards and caused losses each time.

"The fuck do we do? This guy's killin' me." Alan mumbled with closed lips.

Joel leaned over and said, "Miller Lite."

"Fuck that, this guy looks like a friggin' serial killer!"

"Jesus Christ, Slim; be the fuckin' lion for once." Joel said calmly.

"Miller Lite!" Alan turned and yelled as the waitress walked by.

"I got a cold one on the tray, but you can have it." She said as she set the beer on the table to Alan's right.

"Don't be a jerk, tip the girl." Joel said.

"Oh, wait!" He said as he spun around with a red chip in his hand. Without a second thought, he lined up the top of the bottle with the two spots to the left and bumped it with his elbow. Just as Joel said it would, it fell and shot straight across the first and second circles.

"Oh Shit!" Alan said as he turned around.

"Mother fucker!" The guy at first base yelled as he got up.

Alan swallowed as he saw the size of the man when he stood.

"I am so sorry, dude." Alan said, apologetically.

Security had two guards at the table in less than thirty seconds.

The floor went insane as they ran with a towel to dry the two spots. Surveillance watched the video and rewound. They weren't buying it and called down immediately.

"That was intentional." They said.

"We fucking know that!" The pit boss said, then abruptly hung up the phone.

"What do we do." Said Robert.

"Nothing." He responded. "Let it go; this asshole can't stay this lucky forever."

"Not according to Jake."

"Is Jake runnin' this shift?" The pit boss asked angrily.

"No, but he—"

"Good, then pipe down and listen when I'm talkin."

The guy surprisingly avoided a scene and grabbed his chips and left. The game resumed and improved once again. The floor was on pins and needles watching every move and the eye in the sky had their undivided attention.

He was up to over three grand and betting black hundred-dollar chips. The cards were falling in place like lattice wood.

"Maybe I should quit now." Alan said loudly.

"That's up to you man." The dealer said. "I'd quit while was ahead, too."

"Bullshit! We're on a roll, Slim." Joel said.

"I'm two grand up from where I was. Maybe I just got lucky." Alan said.

"One thing you can always be sure about with luck, Mr. Alan," The dealer said, "Sooner or later, it's gonna change."

"What the hell? Fuck that." Joel said. "We gotta long ways to go. Press it."

"Press it?"

"Yeah, Press it, Slim. Go up to two-fifty." Joel said with confidence.

Reluctantly, Alan did as he said, then split a pair of eights. He got dealt low cards on each and doubled on both.

Unfortunately, the small cards kept coming out and he was left with two bad hands and a grand on the table.

"Relax, Slim." Joel said. "He's got a five up."
The dealer turned over a face in the hole and drew another face for a bust.

"Holy Shit!" Alan said, trying to contain his excitement.

"Calm down." Joel said, "They're gonna think somethin's up."

After a while Alan was on top of the world and the excitement had him betting a thousand dollars a hand. The eye in the sky and the entire floor was now on him like a hawk. In a matter of three shuffled shoes he shot up to thirty thousand and started to get cold feet. Outside the evening sun was setting once again.

Suddenly, a hand touched Alan's shoulder and he flinched out of paranoia.

"Excuse me, Mr. Alan?" An attractive dark-haired woman asked with an easy smile and a soothing voice. "I'm a casino host and I'd like to speak with you when you get a chance."

"I do something wrong?" Alan asked as his heart was pounding out of his chest.

"Hey sweetheart!" Joel said. "We're in the middle of a fuckin' play here."

"Nothing's wrong." She said. "They tell me you've been playing here since yesterday."

"Get rid of 'er, Slim!" Joel scoffed as he sat there impatiently. "We don't have time for this shit."

"Can we talk later, ma'am." Alan said rudely over Joel's obnoxious comments. "I'm a little fuckin' busy right now!"

"No problem. Sorry for interrupting but be sure to contact me before ya leave." She said as she slid a business card carefully next to his stacks of chips.

"The hell was that all about?" Alan mumbled to Joel with his hand over his mouth.

"Welcome to the high roller's club, Slim." Joel said. "That hot little number was a host and her job is to kiss your ass and keep you here as long as possible."

"And just what does that entail?" Alan said as he watched her walk away.

As he talked with Joel under his breath, the floor came over to watch closer.

"Cool it, Slim; they're all over us. Just keep facin' forward so the sky don't see us talkin'."

But it was too late, the eye in the sky called down to let them know what was up.

"He's not playing the spreads on a count." The guy in surveillance, said.

"No shit." Said the pit boss. "We know we're being played; his bets aren't fluctuating and he's winning on the first hands out."

"Must be a hell of a streak is all we can figure."

"We'll swap dealers just to be sure there ain't nothing goin' on."

"You better do something quick." He said.

"We're gonna stand over him and hawk him." The floor man said. "I'm raising the table limit too; a streak always turns."

"Ya might wanna wait until—"

The pit boss hung up and raised the limit to five thousand."

"Hit the table limit." Joel said.

"C'mon, Man." Alan said. "That's a lot o' money."

"Just do it." Joel said as he could feel the heat from the floor closing in. "I got ya this far. Trust me, Slim; we're runnin' out o' time."

Reluctantly, he went up to five grand a hand and the pit boss was hanging over the table like a heavy curtain. As Alan carefully watched Joel's signals from the corner of his eye, he played faster, his winnings hit a streak and grew quickly.

Another floor manager walked over and pulled the pit boss away from the table.

"We're too far at a loss, now; around seventy fucking grand." He said, angrily. "This ain't Vegas, we can't afford that kind of loss on one shift."

"What the hell are we supposed to do?" He asked, nervously.

"Keep him in the game, the longer he plays, the more the house edge will creep back in."

As Alan counted his chips and realized how much he had, he began to shake. It was way more than he ever counted on. He broke out in a cold sweat and his heart began to race.

"That's it! Color it up." Alan said, pushing the chips forward.

"Whoa, whoa, whoa!" Joel yelled.

"This is bullshit, I'm not a gambler like Joel Johnson. I'm just a guy trying desperately to get back on track and now I am." Alan said. "I'd be a damn fool to push this kind of luck."

The floor closed in as a bead of sweat rolled down the pit bosses face, knowing that if he quits now and walks with this kind of cash, there would be hell to pay with the casino manager.

"Listen to me, Slim." Joel said slow and calm. "For the love of God, pull the chips back and let's go to the office and talk about this."

Chapter 6. – Reflections.

Alan paced the marble floor of the restroom like a mad man. As he tried calm his nerves to get his heart rate down he looked up and saw Joel standing there cool as ice, lighting a cigarette as if he was patiently waiting for a response.

"Goddammit, Joel." Alan yelled as his voice echoed against the restroom walls. "I can't do this; I gotta quit while I'm ahead."

"Calm down, Slim." Joel said calmly as he exhaled and flicked his ashes in the sink. "This is just how it's done. You have a chance here to get clear."

"I was clear at thirty grand!" He yelled nervously. "I could have lost that, but I kept going--"

"And you won!" Joel yelled. "Ya still got forty over what ya need; we got room to play. Grow some fuckin' balls and take a chance."

"This is fucking ridiculous." Alan snapped, then started washing his face and eyes. "No, better yet, ...this, ...this is fuckin' insane." He added as the warm water washed over his eyes.

"No this is gambling, and as crazy as it sounds, you got one last shot here tonight and you'll never get this chance again. Think about that girl ya got waiting at home. Ain't it worth a shot for her?"

"That, ...just made up my mind, Joel." As Alan wiped his face and looked at Joel through the mirror over his shoulder.

"So what the hell's it gonna be!" Joel said loud enough to echo through the restroom.

"I'm not gonna wind up like you."

Just then a guy walked in the restroom entrance and saw the heated conversation, got spooked and walked back out to avoid any confrontation.

"I don't want you to!" Joel exclaimed, then did a motion like wiping his hands. "After this, you never walk into a casino again."

"Why the hell do you care so damn much anyway?" Alan asked, confused by his persistence.

"I don't know, ...you're the only friend I got?" Joel asked with a quick grin.

Alan looked at him sideways in confusion. Joel had to be either the most complex person he had ever met or literally the most insane; or maybe both.

"Besides," Joel added. "Did you see the fuckin' looks on those bastards faces? They broke the cardinal rule of the house."

"What's that?"

"You made the greedy bastards gamble, and the house never gambles."

Before Alan could respond, a security guard entered the bathroom. Joel and Alan stood there quiet and stared back at him.

"Everything ok in here?" He said with a concerned look on his face. "I'm getting complaints about yelling."

"Everything's fine." Alan said calmly as he walked out leaving Joel behind.

On the way back to the table, the waitress walks quickly over to Alan.

"Mr. Alan" She said. "I just wanted to say thanks for being a friend to Mr. Joel. For years, nobody like him. He always good to me, but he usually just cuss everyone off the tables."

"Yeah, well, maybe it's the drinking." Alan said, while walking. "He's not drinking today though."

"No, he not drinking today." She said. "You need more coffee?"

"No thanks, I'll be gone in a little while."

As Alan walked across the twisted carpet to pit one, he had a sinking feeling as he realized that Jake was back, and he was pissed.

He slowed his pace down and could see a heated argument starting to erupt behind the pitch table. As nerve racking as the day had gone, he never actually faced the realization that he would inevitably return.

He suddenly realized that this may have been the reason Joel had been so anxious and kept pushing him as if they were running out of time.

Nonetheless, with all his chips sitting on the table, there was no way he was going to avoid whatever confrontation he had in store, so he swallowed, took a breath, pulled down his brim and started walking towards the rage that lied ahead.

Chapter 7. – The Wrath of the Floor.

The floor was on pins and needles as Jake's rage was growing like a pressure cooker. He stormed outside of the velvet ropes to the chair where Joel had been sitting and saw the paper sign on Joel's chair.

"After all the bullshit we went through last night, you guys let this shit happen today." Jake said. "And who's the fucking smartass that put that goddamn sign on this chair!"

The Dealer gave a somber look and shrugged as Jake ripped the printed paper sign off the chair, crumpled it up, and dropped it on the carpet.

Alan looked back and spotted Joel walking across the casino floor, then looked back at the floor guys and listened to their vile comments and insults as he reached the table.

"Looks like you had fun while I was gone, Mr. Alan." Jake said angrily with a tensed face while pointing his finger at Alan in disdain. "Just so you know, you color up right now and you're banned. Nobody walks in here, fucks us, and leaves."

"I didn't cheat you guys!" Alan snapped. "Besides, you had no problem taking my damn money."

Jake walked away from the table, but Alan was afraid of what kind of dirty, underhanded trick he would pull now. Joel was right about one thing; this wasn't his 'house', and there were no friends on the opposite side of the table.

Joel walked up, sat down and looked at Alan with disappointment.

"Looks like these assholes rescinded my chair." He said as he leaned over and saw the crumpled paper sign on the floor. "Have to admit, it lasted a lot longer than I thought it would."

Alan took pause and thought again about the whole situation. He knew pressing his luck was not a wise choice. As he stared at the stack of chips, he knew it was peace of mind, but couldn't resist asking, "You, ...you really think I should go for it?"

"You know what I think, Slim." Joel said. "It's up to you. Last chance."

"Ya know what?" Alan said as he pulled his chips in tighter. "Let's roll; we got room to play."

"Now you're talkin', Slim!" Joel said with a quiet roar. "Table limit."

Then a man walked over to the table and stood behind Joel and Alan. It was a fresh shuffle and he was ready to come into the game.

As Alan placed his bet on the square, Joel yelled, "Wait!"

"What?"

"Push it all." Joel said. "Bet the whole fuckin' thing!"

"What! Bet the whole fuckin' thing?" Alan responded as he stared at the large pile of chips.

Jake immediately ran back to the table in a panic.

"Excuse me?" Jake said. "Bet it all?"

"The table limit's only five grand." Alan said as he stared at the chips. "I got seventy fuckin' grand sittin' here."

"You wanna raise the limit?" Jake said, as if he were daring him. "You wanna put it all on the line, go ahead, hot-shot, I'll allow it."

"You can't do that without the casino manager." The dealer quickly interrupted.

"You worry about you're fuckin' job, card jockey and I'll do mine." Jake said as he puffed up at the dealer.

Joel turned and looked at the guy behind him standing there with a hundred-dollar bill in his hand.

"Are you fuckin' kiddin' me!" Joel said.

Then Alan turned and looked at the man.

"You mind if I come in." He asked.

"Hell yeah, he minds you fuckin' jerkoff!" Joel yelled, then turned to Alan. "Tell him to go fuck himself, Slim!"

"If you could, ...just wait until I'm done here, please." Alan pleaded.

Then the guy realized how much money was at stake and looked at Alan and the floor in shock and said, "Whoa, no problem guys."

"Up to you, sir." Jake said, trying to get the guy to come in and upset the flow. "He doesn't own the table." But the guy immediately stepped back and nodded 'no'.

"Do it, Slim." Joel roared. "Be the lion; all in or nothin'!"

"I can't do it; ...I can't go for broke."

"Then go back to bettin' peanuts." Jake said trying to egg Alan on.

With the odds in the house's favor, Jake was willing to take a chance, hoping for the house edge to prevail on a single hand; a gamble that the house never takes.

Alan put five 'thousand-dollar' orange chips in the circle and took a breath. The dealer looked at Alan and was about to pull the first card and said, "All that money and you tip just like cheap ass, Joel Johnson." then looked over at Joel with a disgusted face.

Alan looked at Joel as he sat there and shook his head with a big grin at the dealer.

As the dealer's thumb passed over the deck to pull the card, Alan grabbed his whole pile and shoved it across the table, flooding his circle.

Jake, seeing what happened, ran back to the table.

"That's a lion." Joel said with a grin. "That's a fuckin' lion."

"Did a card come out!" He yelled at the dealer.

"No not yet, we still gotta count and sort it for the bet."

"Fuck that! Deal a goddamn card! Do it now." Jake yelled.

Then immediately, the dealer let a card fly.

"Card's out now, mother fucker! No turning back." Jake said with a huge grin.

"Hope you know what' you're doin'" Said the dealer as he dealt the other face down cards, then turned up a ten of clubs.

"Now that's fuckin' balls to the wall, baby!" Said Joel as he laughed and clapped his hands loudly. "Now we're fuckin' gamblin'! Ya feel that rush!"

"I actually feel kind o' sick." Alan said as he turned up his cards to look at them. He had a hard seventeen. The excitement of the stakes and play started drawing a crowd of players and onlookers behind the table.

"Fuckin' mother-in-law." Alan said with a shaky voice, as he picked up his cards and peeked at them.

"What ya gonna do hotshot?" Jake asked.

"Hit it!" Joel said.

"Hit it?" Alan asked.

"We gotta have a signal." Jake said. "Scrap the cards so he can hit it."

"Yeah, trust me." Joel said. "Last hand, last shot."

"You said, never, *ever*, ...hit a hard seventeen." Alan said in confusion. "Are you insane? I can't hit that shit."

"Then don't!" Jake yelled. "Jesus Christ! Tuck it, but Goddammit, do something."

"Listen to me, Slim." Joel said calmly. "Remember what I told you. This is the devil's house; nothing is as it seems. Trust me, not them. Take the hit."

Alan couldn't believe what Joel was telling him to do. He broke out into a cold sweat as he stared at the dealer's ten as he held a weak, stiff hand. The stack of seventy grand was like a fading salvation that would soon vanish.

Alan took a deep breath, tuned them all out and slowly slid the cards under the stack to stay, but before he let go, at the last second, he pulled it back, twisted his hand and scratched the table with the cards.

"Hit him!" Jake yelled frantically at the dealer.

"And now!" Joel said in a calm voice, "...it's over."

Alan's stomach sank as he knew he had spent all this time to lose everything on one stupid play. "Maybe Joel was part of the smoke and mirrors." He thought as he felt as though he had been played all along and didn't even know it until now. He slowly looked up, and to his complete surprise, there was a beautiful four of hearts sitting in front of him. Although the floor didn't know for sure he was holding a seventeen, Alan, saying he did was proof enough.

The dealer, without thought, flipped his hole card for a sixteen and ironically drew the identical match card from the double deck; the other four of hearts.

As Alan slowly turned his hand over and exposed the 'twenty-one', Jake threw a fit. Alan slammed the hand on the table beside the bet and yelled in relief. The pit phone started ringing and the casino manager quickly showed up. Pandemonium ensued on the floor and the crowd behind Alan erupted in cheers at the sight of such an incredible gamble that doubled seventy grand to a hundred and forty thousand dollars.

"Check the dealer's hole card!" Jake yelled into the phone. "Rewind and check the fuckin' grip of the dealer's top card—"

"We already did, Jake." Surveillance answered. "He wasn't second dealing, the guy just lucked out."

"Bullshit! No one makes a play like that and get's that lucky." Jake yelled.

"Sorry, Jake; tell that to the casino manager; this one's on you guys."

Then the phone hung up on Jake as he threw it on the center pit island.

"Hmm." The dealer chuckled in awe. "He brought the fuckin' house down."

"What now?" Alan asked Joel, as he stared at the large pile of chips being colored and stacked.

"Now you color up; you leave and don't ever come back." Joel said.

"Holy Shit, Joel." Alan said with a crack in his voice. "I had my doubts, but I don't know how to ever thank you. Today, you're my only friend, my *best* friend."

"That's all I needed, Slim." Joel said. "Now I can get the hell out of this fuckin' grind house, too."

"Well hold on!" Alan said, as he reached for his wallet for his player's card, "We're gonna get a couple steaks, and—". As he looked back to his left, Joel had already got up and left.

"Joel?" He said as he looked over to his chair.

Alan stood up and looked all around in confusion, but Joel was nowhere to be seen.

As the dealer continued to count the stacks, Alan noticed he had a slight smug smile on his face.

Suddenly, the floor realized he was going to leave and changed their attitude.

"Mr. Alan, the casino manager said nervously, can we get you anything? Do you have a room? We have some nice suites available."

"Where'd Joel run off to?" Alan asked.

Jake and the casino manager stopped and looked at each other with puzzled expressions.

"What the hell do you mean, 'where did Joel go?'" Jake asked, angrily and perplexed.

"Joel. You know? ...He was sitting right here in his chair."

"No one's been in that chair all day, Mr. Alan." The dealer said in confusion. "We talked about this this morning. I told you we were sorry about what happened."

"What the hell are you guys talkin' about?" Alan asked. "What exactly *did* happen this morning."

"Mr. Alan, ...Joel Johnson dropped dead from a heart attack this morning, not even an hour after you left. Died right there on the floor behind you. We put that sign on that chair out of respect to him. Can't say many people's gonna miss him, but it was the least we could do is keep his chair empty for the day. And he did finally get his sign that he asked for."

With the casino manager, the pit boss, the dealer and several onlookers still behind him, a hush suddenly fell around him so that all that could be heard was the obnoxious ringing of the slots in the background. As they filled a clear tray with high denomination chips, Alan spoke up and broke the silence.

"Out of respect you say?" Alan asked, but only got blank stares back from the crew. "I tell ya what, out of respect to Joel, break down one of those chips. I need two purples for a tip."

"Yes sir, Mr. Alan." The casino manager replied with a smile.

The dealer smiled and obliged and the floor nodded at the gesture, then passed Alan the tray with a hundred and forty grand, including two purple five-hundred dollar chips.

As he stood and stared at the chips, they waited for him to the tip. Alan picked up one of the purple chips and looked at the dealer, then picked up the second and looked at them laying in his palm.

"For the record, ...it was Joel Johnson that brought down the house, ...not me." He said calmly.

Then to their surprise, just as the waitress approached, he closed his hand and held the tip and headed towards the cage. She stopped dead in her tracks and turned with surprise as Alan walked past her and the jingle of two purple chip landed on her tray.

As Alan left the cage and approached the dark tinted double doors of the lobby leading outside of the casino, a voice yelled out behind him to wait.

It was the host that had wanted to talk to him.

"Mr. Alan." She said as she caught her breath. "I am so glad I found you before you left. I've been Joel's host for years; I was the first one to get to him after he collapsed on the floor. He gave me this and said to give it to 'Slim'. I'm pretty sure he meant you."

Then she handed Alan a small bulky envelope. When he opened it, a gold ring with a diamond studded cross fell into his hand.

"You have my card." She said. "Call me if you need anything. And thanks for playing at the Biloxi Royale."

"Thanks, ma'am," Alan said with a nod. "But I don't plan on coming back."

Alan walked through the casino lobby and as he was about to go through the doors leading outside, a security guard ran ahead of him to grab the door, but then Alan realized, he was only opening it for someone coming inside.

THE END.